You Look Like Your Grandpa

by

Raymond C. Fuller, Jr.

Dedication

This book is dedicated to the children who bravely fight cancer every day and to the volunteers with The St. Baldrick's Foundation, shavers and shavees, who have raised millions of dollars to fight alongside the special kids.

Acknowledgements

I probably don't need to, but I acknowledge that I am NOT an artist! Hopefully a future version will have illustrations by a REAL artist!

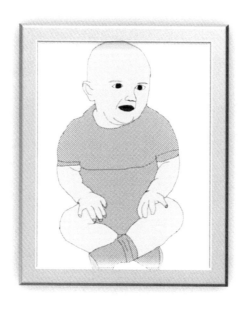

When he was first born, Robbie had no hair at all. But his big brown eyes were just like his grandpa's eyes. Everyone said, "He looks like his grandpa."

When he was little, whenever grandpa took him to the park or to the store, people would greet them and then say to him, "You look like your grandpa." Grandpa loved to hear that. And so did Robbie, because he loved his grandpa. He played with him, read books to him, took long walks with him, made

 bread with him. Grandpa loved spending time with him and he loved spending time with grandpa.

But as he grew older, Robbie didn't like to hear anyone say. "You look like your grandfather."

Grandpa was an old man. He was a boy! Grandpa's hair was gray; his was blond. And Grandpa's ears stuck out; and so did Robbie's.

3

"Grandpa, kids make fun of my ears."

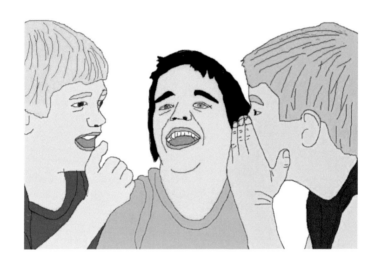

"What do you care about what they think about how you look? It's not important how you look. What's important is who you are."

But it did matter to Robbie, as it does to most kids. He thought if he could grow his hair out, nobody would notice his ears. But his parents kept complaining about his long hair and taking him to get haircuts.

When he asked why, they said that long hair didn't look good on boys. But he kept arguing about it. He even told them, "Grandpa said that I shouldn't care what people think about how I look. What's important is who I am."

His parents told him that he misunderstood what Grandpa had  been trying to say to him, but finally they gave in and they didn't make him cut his hair.

One weekend, Grandpa came by to take Robbie to the movies. Robbie loved going to movies with Grandpa – he always bought popcorn and drinks! And then they usually stopped at a book store and Grandpa would buy him a book or two – or three!

Robbie looked at Grandpa. "Your hair is getting long! You need a haircut!"

But Grandpa just smiled and said, "It's not important how you look. What's important is who you are."

As they bought their tickets, the lady at the counter said to Robbie, "Spending the day with our grandfather?"

"Yeah. How did you know he was my grandfather?"

"You look just like him!"

And that would have been bad enough. But when they bought popcorn, the kid said, "Does your grandson want any butter on his? Man, he looks just like you."

Grandpa just smiled and said, "Thanks." But Robbie wasn't happy.

As they settled into their seats, Robbie turned to his grandpa and said, "Grandpa, I don't want to hurt your feelings, but I don't want to look just like you. I want to look like ME! I want to look different from everyone!"

And of course, Grandpa just smiled and said, "It's not important how you look. What's important is who you are."

Robbie continued to let his hair grow. So did Grandpa. Then one day Grandpa stopped by to take Robbie to a baseball game and Robbie said, "You really need a haircut. Long hair looks silly on an old man."

"But it covers my ears. People don't make fun of my ears anymore."

"Grandpa, I know what you're doing. You're trying to teach me that it's not important how you look. What's important is who you are."

"But how I look is important to you?"

"Yeah, kind of. I mean, I know who you are. But I kind of care about how you look."

"And you don't want to look like me…"

"Well, you've got all those wrinkles and stuff…" Robbie grinned.

"OK, I get your point," Grandpa laughed. "How about when we go to the game today, I pull my hair back and wear a hat?"

"That'll work. And then get a haircut, OK?"

Grandpa laughed, "OK, But…"

"I know, I know. It's not important how you look. What's important is who you are."

Robbie was enjoying the game, but then began to feel funny. His head was hurting again, and now his stomach was upset. He told his grandfather that he wasn't feeling very well and when grandpa looked into his eyes Grandpa decided that maybe they should head home.

Before they could reach the parking lot, Robbie fell to the ground, tripping over nothing. Grandpa realized that something serious was going on and called over to the security guard at the gate who immediately called an ambulance.

A few weeks later, Robbie was still in the hospital. The brain tumor that had been discovered was responding to the chemotherapy, though he still had more treatments before the radiation therapy could begin. The chemicals that were attacking his cancer cells had also caused all of his hair to fall out.

Grandpa came into the room. "Hey, kid! I know everyone wanted you to get a haircut but you kind of went overboard!"

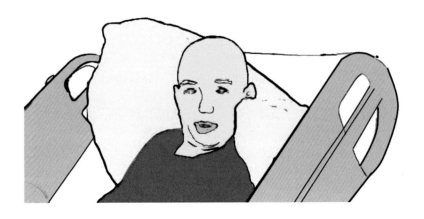

"Very funny, Grandpa." Robbie smiled weakly. "It's not important how you look. What's important is who you are."

"I thought you'd be glad to lose your hair! Now you don't look like anyone you know!"

"Right now, I wish I did. I look awful with no hair."

"And your ears stick out?"

Robbie chuckled again. "Yeah. No kidding!"

"Well, I brought you a hat like mine so you can cover them up!"

"And then I'll look like my grandpa again, huh?"

Grandpa took off his hat, exposing his newly shaved head.

"You know it kid. You know it."

19

Please consider making a donation to The St. Baldrick's Foundation, "a volunteer-driven charity committed to funding the most promising research to find cures for childhood cancers and give survivors long and healthy lives."

http://www.stbaldricks.org/

20

28252767R00017

Made in the USA
Lexington, KY
11 January 2019